Bye-bye fear: God is here!

By: Jolene A. Feist

WestBow Press books may be ordered through booksellers or by contacting:

WestBow Press
A Division of Thomas Nelson & Zondervan
1663 Liberty Drive
Bloomington, IN 47403
www.westbowpress.com
844-714-3454

Title page:
Illustrated by: Bill Ross & Jane Luna

NLT:
• Scripture quotations marked (NLT) are taken from the Holy Bible, New Living Translation, copyright ©1996, 2004, 2015 by Tyndale House Foundation. Used by permission of Tyndale House Publishers, a Division of Tyndale House Ministries, Carol Stream, Illinois 60188. All rights reserved.

ISBN: 978-1-6642-7557-7 (sc)
ISBN: 978-1-6642-7559-1 (hc)
ISBN: 978-1-6642-7558-4 (e)

Library of Congress Control Number: 2022915161

Print information available on the last page.

WestBow Press rev. date: 08/19/2022

WESTBOW
PRESS®
A DIVISION OF THOMAS NELSON
& ZONDERVAN

Description: "Bye-bye fear; God is here" is a story of a toddler boy named Eli who is learning to overcome his fears with God's help. His mommy and daddy teach him to say, "bye-bye fear; God is here!" Saying this helps him feel more confident so that he can face his fears.

First, he overcomes his fear that his parents will leave him alone in the church nursery. Then, when he has a doctor's appointment, he is afraid to have his ears and throat checked; Eli faces that fear too. He overcomes his fears of the shaky bridge at the park, and the big swimming pool he visits with his cousins.

Soon, he feels brave enough to climb the brick wall in the backyard, and he even helps his mommy conquer her own fear of snakes. With God's help, Eli and all the other children of the world can overcome their fears. If you are a Christian parent and you want to say goodbye to fear in your children's lives, you have chosen the right book. God does not want our children to live in fear, and it is our job as parents to raise our children in the ways of the Lord and teach them that with the Lord's help, they can overcome all their fears. We should be the strongest example in teaching our children to be fearless, and God will even teach us through our children to conquer all our fears as we surrender our children to the Lord.

Dear readers,

This book is dear to me because much of the story lines are true events that happened with my oldest son. I have personally struggled with different fears throughout my life until 2021 when I finally got to the place of being sick and tired of feeling afraid being a young Mom. I had to get to the place of fully surrendering my children to the Lord and this is when the victory came. There are so many different fears that can creep in as parents, but God calls us to not fear and to trust him by walking in faith. There are over 365 bible verses for us to read in the Bible that deal with fear. For the Christian parent, I believe it is extremely important to first receive victory over fear in our own life before we can help kick it out of our children's lives! Through much prayer, scripture memory, and repetition of the simple phrase, "bye-bye fear, God is here" I was able to help my kids overcome fear and that's when I began to see changes in my kids' lives. Fear is an epidemic right now and we need to kick fear out of our homes and raise fearless young warriors!

We pray as you read "Bye-bye fear, God is here" with your children that it touches your heart and helps your Children to walk in faith and not fear. Be blessed and enjoy our story.

"For God has not given us a spirit of fear and timidity, but of power, love, and self-discipline." –2 Timothy 1:7 NLT

Jolene Feist

As For me and this house we will serve the Lord. Joshua 24 15

Once upon a time, there was a strong young boy named Eli. Eli was learning to overcome all his fears with God's help. He loved Jesus, loved to sing to Jesus, and even started learning to pray to Jesus.

Every time Eli would get closer to God, fear would always seem to be right around the corner. His mommy and daddy taught him to say, "Bye-bye fear; God is here!"

Eli absolutely loved going to church. He loved getting ready for church and picking out his outfit with Mommy. He sang to Jesus all the way to church.

He loved seeing his friends at church and playing with all the fun toys, but it was always hard to say goodbye to Mommy and Daddy. Daddy said to Eli, "bye-bye fear! God is here!" Those words comforted Eli, and he began to play with his friends at church.

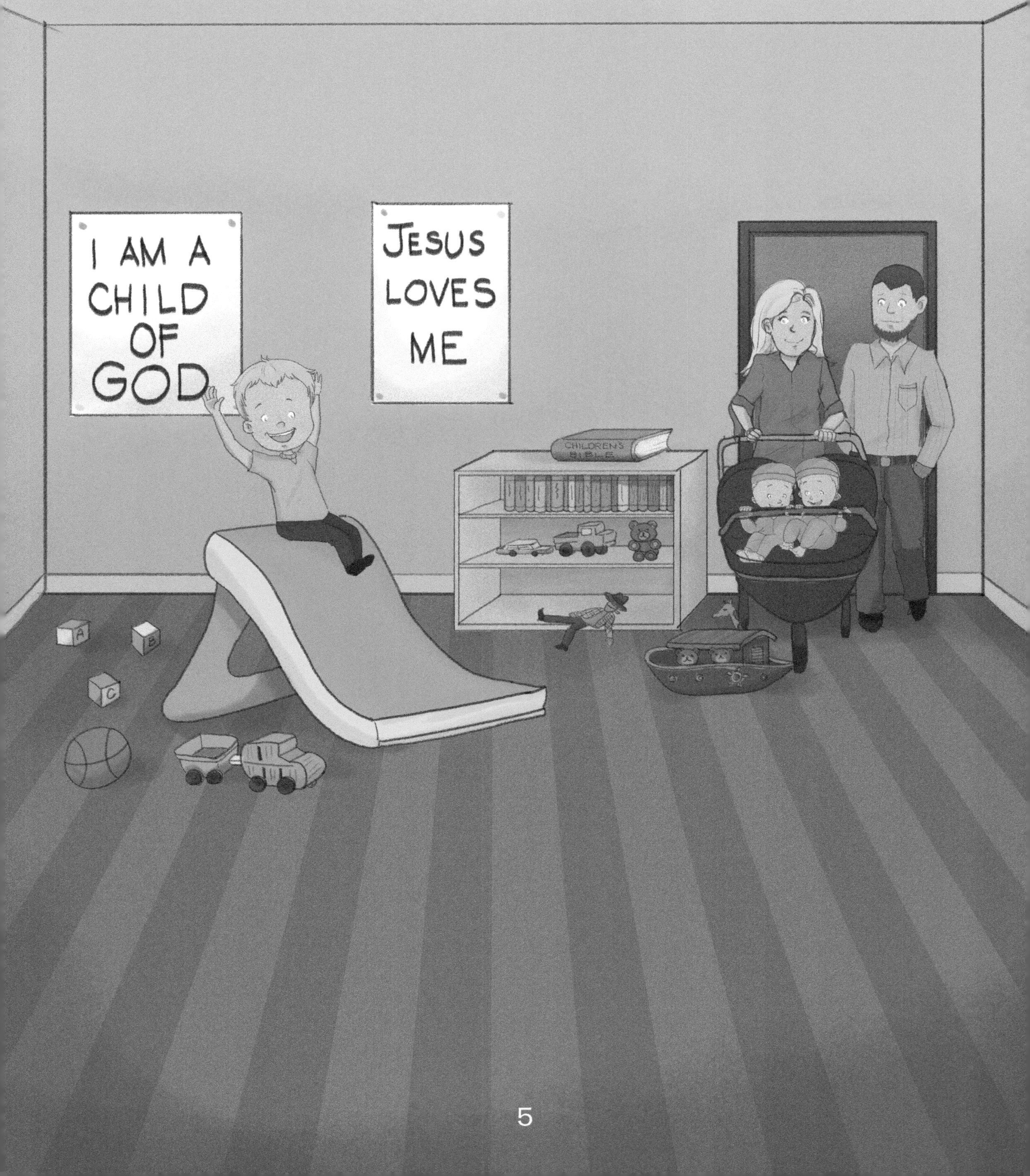
I AM A CHILD OF GOD
JESUS LOVES ME
CHILDREN'S BIBLE

Eli had so much fun at church. He played on the slide, played with his cars and puzzles and had many giggles. His friends started to leave because their mommies and daddies came to pick them up. Eli realized his mommy and daddy were not there yet, so he remembered to pray, "Bye-bye fear! God is here!" When Mommy and Daddy picked Eli up, they were so happy to see that he was not afraid.

Eli beat the fear of being away from mommy and daddy!

For God has not given us a spirit of fear and timidity, but of power, love, and self-discipline. 2 Timothy 1:7 NLT

Eli had to go to the doctor for a yearly check up with Mommy and Daddy. The doctor was always so nice, but Eli was nervous. He was afraid to get his ears and throat checked and started to cry. Mommy and Daddy both whispered to Eli, "Bye-bye fear! God is here!"

Eli calmed down and listened to the doctor the rest of the time and did what the doctor asked. He did such a good job that the doctor gave him a sticker!

Eli beat the fear of going to the doctor!

This is my command—be strong and courageous! Do not be afraid or discouraged. For the Lord your God is with you wherever you go. Joshua 1:9 NLT

Eli loved going to the park; it was one of his favorite things to do. He loved walking to the park with Mommy, Daddy and his brothers.

He loved going down the slides, but in order to get to the slide, Eli had to walk across the shaky bridge. He looked at Mommy and said, "Can you hold my hand?"

Mommy came up and held his hand. She whispered, "Bye-bye fear; God is here!"

All of a sudden, a big group of kids arrived at the park. They started running across the bridge and climbing up the bars. Eli smiled at them and became confident. He started running across the bridge with them and even climbing up the bars. This made Mommy and Eli so happy because he overcame his fear.

Eli beat the fear of heights!

I am leaving you with a gift-peace of mind and heart. And the peace I give is a gift the world cannot give. So don't be troubled or afraid. John 14:27 NLT

Eli went with his cousins to a big swimming pool; he had never been to one before. He was scared to go into the pool. Mommy told Eli, "Bye-bye fear! God is here!"

Eli remembered that God was with him, and then he had the confidence to jump in the pool with his cousins. This was one of his favorite days of the summer. Eli beat another fear!

Eli beat the fear of the big swimming pool!

I prayed to the Lord, and he answered me.
He freed me from all my fears. Psalm 34:4 NLT

Eli was getting to be so brave that he even learned how to climb a brick wall in the backyard. This made Mommy afraid. She had to say under her breath, "Bye-bye fear; God is here!"

16

Eli is so fearless now that he even helps his mommy beat her own fear of snakes!

Then Eli started to pick some of his neighbor's flowers through the fence. Mommy said, "No, Eli, you can't pick those." Then she heard a hiss and saw a snake slithering away from Eli. Mommy jumped and shouted, "Come on, Eli; let's leave the fence!" Then Mommy was so afraid again, so she had to whisper to herself, "Bye-bye fear; God is here!" Mommy knew that she had some fears she needed to conquer that day. Mommy said to Eli, "Even mommies and daddies have to pray to God when they get afraid."

Sometimes Eli was afraid to sleep by himself in his own bed and wanted to sleep in Mommy and Daddy's bed. But because Eli had such a strong confidence that God was with him, he looked at Mommy and Daddy and said, "Bye-bye fear; God is here!"

In peace I will lie down and sleep, for you alone, O LORD, will keep me safe. Psalm 4:8 NLT

You can go to bed without fear; you will lie down and sleep soundly. Proverbs 3:24 NLT

Mommy and Daddy were so proud of Eli and all the fears he conquered during the summer. Mommy and daddy gave him a hug and said, "God is so happy with you, Eli. Let's pray right now for all the other children in the world to conquer their fears as well."

Dear Lord,

We pray for every child in the world. You made them and love them and know every detail about them, even their struggles and fears. God, we pray for peace, and we pray for all their fears to leave them, in Jesus Mighty name. We also pray for their salvation and hope that they will draw close to you and know that you are near to them. Amen!

Lightning Source UK Ltd.
Milton Keynes UK
UKHW051000270223
417719UK00009B/92